Do Not Step On The Ant!

Casey L Adams

Aryla Publishing © 2017

www.arylapublishing.com

Visit the site for more information on books by <u>Casey Adams</u> *and to be informed of* **free promotions!**

For my daughter who has a fear of bugs we are working through it one ant at a time ☺

If you enjoy this book I would really appreciate it if you could please leave me an honest review. Please also visit my author page to get more books in this gooey series.

Casey Adams Books

Body Goo 1 **Sneezing**

Body Goo 2 **Burping**

Body Goo 3 **Farting**

Body Goo 4 **Vomiting**

Body Goo 5 **The Crusty Bits**

Body Goo 6 **The Sticky Bits**

Love Bugs **Don't Step in The Ant**

Love Bugs **Don't Splat the Spider**

Please Sign Up to my email list to get information about my new releases and free promotions

Adam hated bugs! Creepy, crawly, flying, stinging, biting bugs, he hated them all. Oh, but ants were the worst, he especially hated ants. He found them everywhere. In his toy box, under his bed, in his closet, on the patio under the picnic table, they were everywhere!

One day, Mom took Adam for a walk in the park. It was a warm and sunny summer afternoon. The sun was shining bright in the sky, the ducks were slowing swimming in the nearby pond and the ants were crawling all over the walkway. Adam was horrified. The ants were everywhere!

He decided that he would play a game. How many ants could he stomp on? He began jumping up and down, first with both feet, then one at a time. He was having loads of fun when suddenly his mom grabbed his arm and shouted, "Stop that! Do not step on the ants!"

"That is not very nice, Adam," his mom said.

"Ants are just as important as we are, and they have feelings too. Don't you know that ants are also very important to the environment?"

"They're just ants," Adam said. "Creepy little crawly bugs."

"Just because something is smaller than you and you don't understand it, doesn't mean that it's not important," Mom said. "Ants are very important to the environment. They are farmers, they dig in the soil and plant seeds. If it were not for ants, we would never have all these beautiful flowers and trees. Ants also keep other insects like flies and bees away. You should be glad that we have ants around."

"Humph. I still don't like ants," Adam mumbled, "Not one little bit."

That night after his mom tucked him into bed and turned out the light, Adam began to feel funny.

He felt a tingle from the top of his head to the tip of his big toe.

But he was too sleepy to worry about it and quickly fell asleep.

The next morning Adam woke up and things looked weird. He was not on top of his bed, he was under it and the bed was gigantic, much bigger than he remembered. He ran across the floor as fast as he could, and he wondered why it seemed to take him such a long time to reach the big mirror on his closet door.

AAAHHHH! What happened? Adam was an ant! A tiny, creepy, crawly ant. Before he could even gather his thoughts, a huge foot stepped through the door and almost squashed him flat. It was his mother, coming to wake him up for school. He screamed and hollered as loud as he could, but she didn't hear even a peep because he was so small. Adam ran as fast as his little ant legs could carry him.

He made it back under the bed just as his Mom walked by.

He leaned against the wall to catch his breath when someone grabbed his arm and pulled him right through a small crack.

AAHHHH! It was another ant. "Hey, the boss is looking for you," the ant said. "You are late for work."

"Work?" Adam replied.

"We're on a tight deadline. We have to finish the new tunnel by nightfall."

"Tunnel?" Adam gulped.

"Come on!" The other ant grabbed his arm and pulled him through a tiny crack in the floor. They went through a dark, narrow tunnel for what seemed like miles, until it finally opened up into a large cave, with dozens of tunnels running from every wall.

Adam stood in disbelief as he stared at the huge cave that was just beneath his house.

Some were carrying food, some were digging in the tunnels, and some were directing the others where to go.

"Go all the way to the end and start digging," the ant ordered. Adam ran to the end of the tunnel and started digging furiously in the hard dirt.

"Hey, slow down, amigo." Another ant tapped him on the shoulder. The other ant was much larger than Adam and the other black ants. He spoke with a Spanish accent. "You do not have to work yourself to death."

"Who are you?" Adam asked.

"My name is Miguel, and I'm from Argentina," the other ant replied.

"How did you get to America?" Adam asked.

"I hitched a ride in some luggage," Miguel said. "It was a long, hot trip and I was really glad when it was over."

"Why is this tunnel so important?" Adam asked.

"There must be at least a hundred tunnels down here."

"You're new to this life, aren't you?" Miguel asked

"You could say that," Adam replied. "I haven't been around very long."

"Well, ants have to constantly build new tunnels," Miguel explained. "Predators always manage to find our tunnels and we don't not want them invading the colony."

"Predators?" Adam asked.

"Mostly, spiders, lizards, and other ants. We cannot let just anyone enter the nest," Miguel said. "We need new tunnels so we can keep food coming in for the queen and the colony as well. Plus, we also need them in case we need to make a hasty retreat in the event of an invasion."

"Wow, I never knew that ants had such a hard life," Adam said.

"Yes, and we have to pack as much work in as we can," Miguel said. "We only live about four months after all."

"FOUR MONTHS!" Adam shouted. "Ants only live four months? Then what happens?"

"We die," Miguel said. "You really are new at this, aren't you?"

"I don't think I like being an ant," Adam said. "I want to go back to being a little boy again."

Suddenly, the ground began to shake violently and dirt fell all around Adam and Miguel. The other ants in the tunnel scattered into any hole they could find.

"What is happening?" Adam yelled. "Is it an earthquake?" He and Miguel ran to the end of the tunnel and peered around the corner.

The cave was completely empty except for a few large black ants holding sticks and hiding behind rocks.

"I do not think this is an earthquake," Miguel said. "Look." He pointed toward the entrance to one of the tunnels a few yards away. Dust, smoke, and rocks billowed from the tunnel. Adam watched in horror as thousands and thousands of large black and red ants came charging through the middle of the cave. "Army ants!" Miguel said.

"What are they doing?" Adam asked, hiding behind Miguel's larger body.

"It looks like the entire colony is on the move," Miguel said. "When they decide to change locations the whole colony goes, and they destroy anything and everything in their path."

"Will they eat us?" Adam asked.

"They don't look hungry to me," Miguel replied. "But stay hidden just in case. Army ants will eat just about anything. We'll have to close that tunnel when this is over. Looks like it will be a long night."

After what seemed like hours, the army ants were all gone and the colony slowly began to come out of hiding. Several tunnels had collapsed and the room where all the food had been stored was empty. The army ants had stolen all of their food supplies.

"We need to get that new tunnel finished quickly," a large black ant shouted. "You worker ants get busy and get that tunnel open, then get out there and bring in more food. Carpenters. Get that old tunnel closed before a spider finds it."

"Spider?" Adam said.

"Spiders are an ant's worst enemy," Miguel replied. "If a spider finds an opening into the nest, it will eat us all."

"Ugh!" Adam said with a shiver. "I really don't like being an ant."

Adam and Miguel followed a group of ants into the new tunnel and dug as fast as they could until they broke through to the outside world.

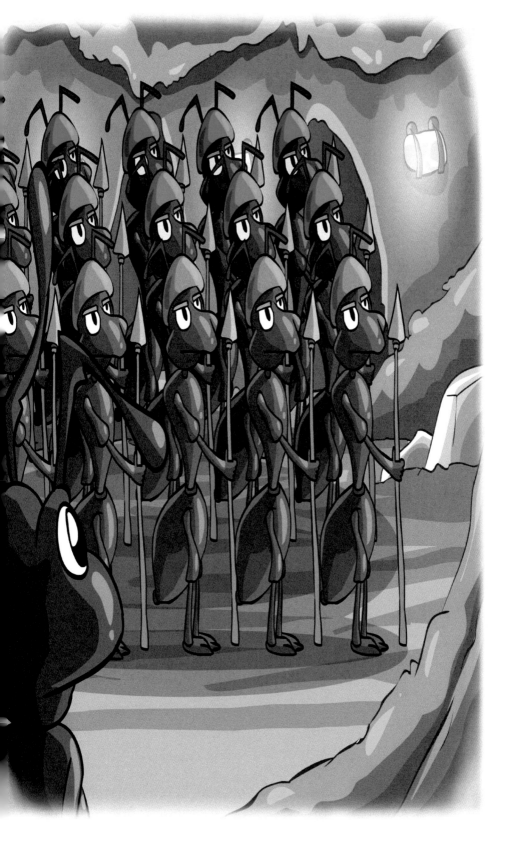

Adam recognized his backyard immediately. His swing set, his tree house in the big maple tree, and the half-eaten peanut butter and jelly sandwich he had left on the patio the day before.

"Help me carry that sandwich back to the nest," Adam said to Miguel. "It is much too big for me to carry alone."

"Do not be silly," Miguel said. "You are an ant, you can lift fifty times your own weight. You take it back to the nest while I go and hunt for more food." Adam ran to the patio and looked up at the half-eaten sandwich. It was huge, much bigger than he was. Miguel must be the silly one, he thought. There is no way a tiny ant could lift a big piece of sandwich like that.

He walked around and around the sandwich, trying to think of a way to get it back to the nest. Maybe I can push it, he thought to himself. Rubbing his hands together, he took a deep breath and pushed with all his might.

To his surprise, the sandwich slid across the patio and into the grass.

"That was easy," Adam thought, "I'm like Superman." Flexing his muscles, he admired his tiny muscular arms.

"Stop playing around," Miguel shouted coming up from right behind him. He was carrying an apple with a bite taken out of it. "We need to get this food back to the nest before nightfall when the spiders come out."

Suddenly the ground began to shake. "Army ants again?" Adam asked.

"Worse," Miguel said. "Spiders, and they must be hungry." Adam looked behind him, and to his horror saw two huge brown spiders coming fast. "Grab the sandwich and let's go."

Adam picked up the sandwich with ease, then he and Miguel ran as fast as they could back to the nest with the food they had found.

"Seal the tunnel, seal the tunnel!" Miguel screamed, as he and Adam dove through the opening. The worker ants quickly began filling the tunnel opening with dirt and rocks. As one of the spiders ran into the freshly built wall with a thud, Adam saw his huge, black eye peering through the small opening before the worker ants sealed it shut.

"That was close," Miguel said. "I thought we were spider chow for sure." Adam was still shaking from the experience, having never been chased by a spider before. If he were still a boy, he would have just squashed those spiders where they stood, but, as an ant, he was much smaller than they were. He hated being an ant more than ever now, but, he had discovered a new found respect for them. He vowed that if he ever became a boy again, he would never step on another ant as long as he lived.

At the end of the day, the ants had filled the storeroom with enough food to feed the whole colony for a few days, and the tunnels had been sealed up so that no spiders could find their way in during the night.

Miguel and Adam sat down to rest after a hard day's work. "Get a good night's sleep Adam," Miguel said. "We have a lot more work to do in the morning." But, Adam was really tired, and so sleepy that he didn't hear anything that Miguel was saying. He fell right to sleep.

RRIIIIINNGG!!! Adam jumped up, frightened at first, thinking a spider may have gotten into the nest and was feasting on his new ant friends. But, to his surprise, he was in his own bed! He was back in his own bedroom, in his own house.

He ran to the mirror and saw that he was a boy again. He felt his face and legs, looking closely at his fingers and toes. He was indeed fully human again.

"Adam!" His mom was standing at his door. "Glad to see you are up early."

"I had a horrible nightmare last night," he said. "I dreamed I was an ant and lived underneath the house in tunnels with thousands of other ants. I had to help dig tunnels, and bring food back to the nest, and I was almost eaten by spiders."

"That sounds horrible," his mom said, as she patted him on the head and pulled a strand of grass from his hair and handed it to him.

"Better wash your hair before you get ready for school."

Adam stared at the strand of grass. "It was just a dream, right?"

As his mom walked him to school that morning, he noticed an ant crawling across the sidewalk, headed toward a piece of candy that someone had dropped.

"STOP!" Adam yelled, and stepped in front of his mom.

"Adam! What is wrong?" she said.

"Do not step on the ant!" he said. He reached down and picked up the candy, carefully placing it on the little ant. "There you go little ant, take that back to the nest, and watch out for those spiders.

The End

A word from the Author

Thank you for reading my book. I sincerely hope you enjoyed it! ☺

I would love it if you could leave me an honest review on what you thought of this book.

If you enjoyed this book you will also like other books in this series........

You can read in any order

If you like to know more about my books and the opportunity to be notified of free promotions please visit http://www.caseyadamsbooks.com

Thank you

Casey

Please visit Aryla Publishing for more books by Casey L Adams and other great Authors. Sign up to be informed of upcoming free book promotions and a chance to win prizes in our monthly prize draw.

Or visit www.ArylaPublishing.com

My website www.CaseyAdamsBooks.com

Follow me on Facebook Twitter and Instagram @arylapublishing

Thank you for your support!

Other children series published by Aryla Publishing

Author Pamela Malcolm

Billy Go To Bed

Billy Get Ready For School

Billy Brush Your Teeth

Billy Eat Your Veg

Billy Tidy Up Your Toys

Billy Go To Bed

Billy Get Ready For School

Billy Brush Your Teeth

Billy Eat Your Veg

Billy Tidy Up Your Toys

Billy's Halloween

Billy's Fireworks Night

Billy's Christmas

Billy's Day Out In London

Billy's Easter Egg Hunt

Ruby Won't Use Her Potty!

Ruby's New Shoes

Ruby Goes Christmas Shopping

Ruby No More Binky (Dummy)

Fiona Fire Engine

Percy Police Car

Made in the USA
Monee, IL
13 July 2020